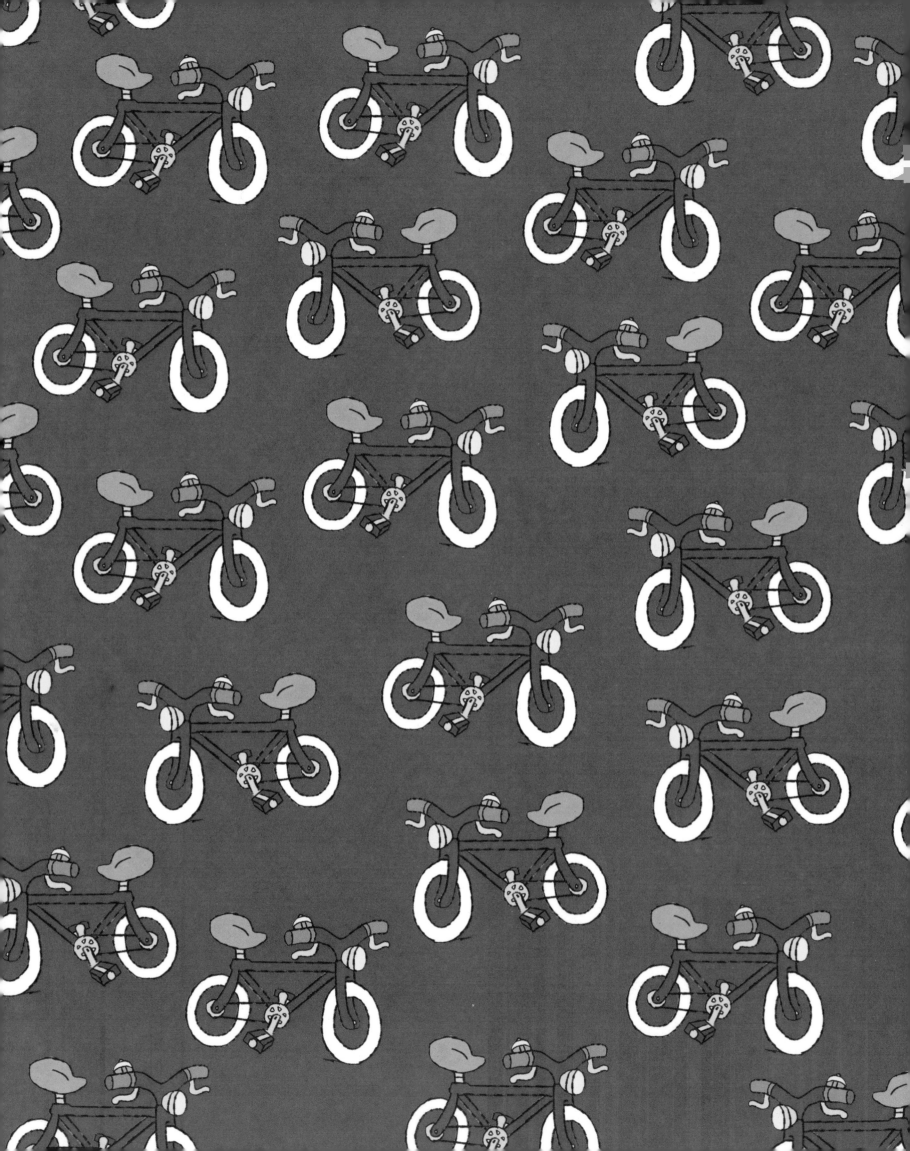

Kate McMullan

BULLDOG'S BIG DAY

HELP
WANTED

- FIREFIGHTER
- WINDOW WASHER
- SIGN PAINTER
- BOOKSELLER

DOG

PICTURES BY

Pascal Lemaitre

ORCHARD BOOKS / NEW YORK / AN IMPRINT OF SCHOLASTIC INC.

Library of Congress Cataloging-in-Publication Data

McMullan, Kate.

Bulldog's big day / Kate McMullan ; pictures by Pascal Lemaitre. —1st ed.   p. cm.

Summary: While looking for a job, Bulldog tries being a firefighter, a window washer, a sign painter,

and a bookseller before finding just the right job for him.

ISBN 978-0-545-17155-7

[1. Occupations—Fiction. 2. Bulldogs—Fiction. 3. Dogs—Fiction. 4. Animals—Fiction.]

I. Lemaitre, Pascal, ill. II. Title. PZ7.M47879Bu 2011 [E]—dc22 2010026235

10 9 8 7 6 5 4 3 2 1   11 12 13 14 15

First edition, February 2011

Printed in Singapore   46

The artwork was created using pen and ink, colored in Adobe Photoshop.

The text was set in Folio Medium. The display type was set in MotterCorpusEF.

Book design by Marijka Kostiw

For Orly Lindgren

and Scarlett Lindgren

—K.M.

For Christina Sterner

and Steve Poses

—P.L.

WAKE UP, EVERYBODY!

All around town,
alarm clocks are ringing and singing,
beeping and buzzing.

Spider wakes up hungry for a bug.

"Oh, my wrinkly knees!"
exclaims Elephant.
"It's time to get up!"

Moose has been up since dawn, painting a sign.

Giraffe's alarm clock sounds like a fire truck backing up: *beep-beep-beep-beep!*

Everybody's up!
Everybody but Bulldog.

EXCITING HUSTLE-BUSTLE

Ring! Ring!
In Bulldog's dream,
the phone is ringing.
"Hello?"

Bulldog gets up. He scrubs his
bulldog face and brushes his
bulldog teeth.

He puts on his
bulldog sweater.

At breakfast,
Bulldog reads the
HELP WANTED ads,
but there are no jobs
for a helpful bulldog.

So Bulldog bakes a batch
of bulldog cookies.

Ding!
Cookies are done.

Bulldog puts them
out to cool.

Outside, everyone is yakking and laughing and rushing off to work.

"Taxi!" bellows Elephant. "TAXI!"
All the hustle-bustle looks exciting!

Today will be my BIG DAY!
thinks Bulldog.
I will find a job.

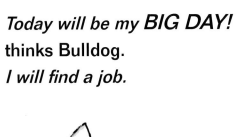

HELP WANTED

- FIREFIGHTER
- WINDOW WASHER
- SIGN PAINTER
- BOOKSELLER

Bulldog packs
his bulldog bag
(with cookies)
and goes outside.

OFF TO WORK!

Next to his house,
Bulldog spies a sign.

Firefighter—that's the job for me!
Bulldog jumps on his bulldog bicycle
and rides off to the firehouse.

Meanwhile . . .
Giraffe's friend gives him
a lift to work.

Spider loves a subway ride.

Moose admires a sign as he waits for the bus.

Elephant is stuck in traffic.
Will she be LATE for work?

BULLDOG THE FIREFIGHTER

At the firehouse, the firefighters are busy washing the fire truck.

"I would like to be a firefighter," says Bulldog.
"Excellent!" says Giraffe.
"You can start as Ladder Truck Checker."
He gives Bulldog a screwdriver, a wrench, and a firefighter's hat.

Bulldog opens the hood of the ladder truck.
He has never seen such a shiny engine!
In fact, he has never seen any engine at all.
He tightens the screws and bolts.
Tuned up!

There are levers on the ladder truck.
Bulldog must check to make sure they work.
He pulls the first lever DOWN.
The ladder rises up from the truck.
He pulls the second lever DOWN.
The ladder rises higher.
He pulls the third lever DOWN. . . .

UH-OH, BULLDOG!

The ladder goes
UP through the ceiling,
UP through the
firefighters' kitchen,
UP
UP
UP.

"Snap my suspenders!"
cries Fire Chief Giraffe.
"It's goin' through the roof!"

The firefighters lower the ladder.
"Bulldog," says Giraffe,
"Firefighter is not the job for you."

Bulldog gives back the screwdriver,
the wrench, and the firefighter's hat.
"Have a cookie," he says.
"Thank you!" says Giraffe.

BARRRRRRMP! BARRRRRRRMP!
The fire alarm is blasting!
The firefighters peel out onto the street, sirens blaring:
WHAAAAAOOOOOOOOOOOAAAAAAAAOOOOO!
They honk their horns:
BEEEEEEEEEP! BEEEEEEEEEP!
Bulldog watches the truck race off.

Window washer, thinks Bulldog.
That's the job for me!
He jumps on his bulldog bicycle
and rides to Window Washer Headquarters.

BULLDOG THE WINDOW WASHER

"I would like to be a window washer,"
says Bulldog.
"Cool," says Spider.
"You can start as Assistant Soaper."

He gives Bulldog a bucket,
a rag, a strap, and a
window washer's belt.

Bulldog and Spider ride the bus
to a tall office building.

They take the elevator up to the top floor.

Bulldog fills his bucket with soapy water.

Spider helps Bulldog attach the strap to his window washer's belt.

He opens the window and clips the ends of the strap to hooks outside the window.

"Ready?" asks Spider.
"Ready!" says Bulldog.
He steps out onto the window ledge.

UH-OH, BULLDOG!

YAAAAOWIE!
The ground is
WAAAAAY
down there.

"Start soaping!"
calls Spider.
But Assistant
Soaper Bulldog
is frozen with fear.

"Oh, my sticky feet!"
cries Spider.

He crawls out
onto the
window ledge
and slowly,
slowly
leads
Bulldog
back inside.

"Whew!" says Bulldog.
"Bulldog," says Spider,
"Window washer is not the job for you."
Bulldog gives back the bucket, the rag,
the strap, and the window washer's belt.

He watches Spider wash the
windows.

Bulldog and Spider
go back to
Window Washer
Headquarters.

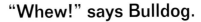

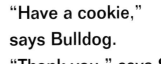

"Have a cookie,"
says Bulldog.
"Thank you," says Spider.

Sign painter, thinks Bulldog.
That's the job for me!
He jumps on his bulldog bicycle
and rides to the
SIGNS studio.

BULLDOG THE SIGN PAINTER

"I would like to be
a sign painter," says Bulldog.
"Beautiful!" says Moose.
"You can start as my
Brush Pot and Sign Holder."

Moose gives Bulldog
a smock, a beret, and
a brush pot.

"I will paint a sign for
Flora's Flowers," says Moose.
He sets out lots of flowers.
Bulldog takes a sniff. *Sweet!*

Moose starts painting.
"New brush!" he calls.
Bulldog holds out the brush pot.
Moose takes a brush and keeps painting.
Bulldog holds the canvas still until . . .
his nose begins to tickle.

"Ah, Moose?" says Bulldog.
"Not now!" says Moose.
The tickle keeps tickling.

"Ah . . . ah . . . Moose?" says Bulldog.
"Shhhh!" says Moose. "Artist at work!"
The tickle is too much for Bulldog.
"Ah . . . ah . . . AH . . . **AH . . .** "

UH-OH, BULLDOG!

"...*CHOOOOOOOOOOOOOOOOOO!*"
The sneeze sends Moose's canvas sailing.
"Oh, my drippin' antlers!" cries Moose.

Bulldog knocks over the paint.
Brushes go flying!
Bulldog runs to pick them up,
leaving bulldog paw prints.

Bulldog helps Moose clean up his studio.
"Bulldog," says Moose,
"Sign painter is not the job for you."
Bulldog gives back his smock and his beret.
"Have a cookie," he says.
"Mmm, thank you," says Moose.

Bookseller! thinks Bulldog.
No ladders,
no high ledges,
no messy paint.
That's the job for me!
He jumps on his bulldog bicycle
and rides to the bookshop.

BULLDOG THE BOOKSELLER

"I would like to be a bookseller,"
says Bulldog.
"Smart choice!" says Elephant.
"You can start as Book Shelver."
She gives him a name tag
that says BULLDOG.

Bulldog gets to work opening boxes
and putting books on the shelves.

He picks up a book with a bulldog on the cover,
MAX: BULLDOG DETECTIVE.
Bulldog begins to read.

. . . a bad cat is stealing all the dog biscuits.

Why would a cat want dog biscuits?
Max asks himself.
Purr-haps it is not a cat at all,
but a dog in disguise.

Bulldog keeps reading.
What will happen next?

UH-OH, BULLDOG!

Bulldog turns the page.
He does not see Elephant standing over him.

"Bulldog?" says Elephant.
"Wait," says Bulldog.
"Bulldog!" says Elephant.
"Two more pages!" says Bulldog.
"BULLDOG!" bellows Elephant.
"Finished!" Bulldog closes the book.
"What a good story!"

"Oh, my wrinkly knees!" cries Elephant.
"We have work to do."
Elephant and Bulldog shelve
the books together.

"Bulldog," says Elephant,
"Bookseller is not the job for you."
Bulldog gives back his name tag.
"Have a cookie," he says.
"Well, maybe just six or seven," says Elephant.

Bulldog climbs onto his bulldog bicycle.
Today was not my BIG DAY after all,
he thinks as he rides slowly home.

THE LAST BULLDOG COOKIE

Bulldog stops under the sign.
*Not one of these
was the job for me*, he thinks.

Inside his bulldog house,
Bulldog opens his bulldog bag
and finds one last bulldog cookie.
He nibbles it, feeling sad.
He will never be a part
of the exciting hustle-bustle.

A knock sounds.
Bulldog opens the door.
"Hello, Bulldog!" say Giraffe, Spider,
Moose, and Elephant.
"Do you have any more of those
excellent cookies?" says Giraffe.
"Cool cookies," says Spider.
"Beautiful cookies!" says Moose.
"I could eat a ton of 'em," says Elephant.

"Come back tomorrow,"
says Bulldog.

BULLDOG'S BIG DAY

The next morning,
Bulldog puts on a baker's apron
and a baker's hat.

He whips up a quadruple-quintuple
batch of bulldog cookies.

Outside, everyone is
yakking and laughing
and waiting in a long, long line.
Bulldog smiles.
All the exciting hustle-bustle
has come to him!

TODAY is my BIG DAY!
thinks Bulldog.
I have found the job for me!

Bulldog runs outside and welcomes his customers to the Grand Opening of Bulldog's Cookie Bakery!

BULLDOG'S OATMEAL-CARROT COOKIES *

Here's my latest BULLDOG COOKIE recipe.
These cookies don't have egg in them, so when you're
finished, you can lick the batter off your paws.
You can lick the spoon. You can even lick the bowl!

Here's what you'll need to bake them:

1 cup white or whole wheat pastry flour

1 cup rolled oats

1 teaspoon baking powder

½ teaspoon salt

½ cup chopped walnuts

1¼ cups shredded carrots

½ cup maple syrup

½ cup unrefined coconut oil

1 teaspoon grated ginger

Here's what to do:

1. Preheat your oven to 375 degrees Fahrenheit.
2. Line two baking sheets with parchment paper.
3. Combine the flour, oats, baking powder, and salt in a big bowl. Stir them together.
4. Add the nuts and carrots. Stir some more.
5. In a smaller bowl, combine the maple syrup, coconut oil, and ginger. Stir them together.
6. Pour the liquid from the smaller bowl into the big bowl. Stir until all the ingredients are combined.
7. Using a tablespoon, drop the batter onto the cookie sheets. Don't crowd the cookies!
8. Bake the cookies for 12–15 minutes or until the edges begin to brown.
9. Take your cookies out of the oven and let them cool.

I love making BULLDOG COOKIES. I hope you will, too!

This recipe was adapted from one found on www.101cookbooks.com.

* PLEASE DO NOT ATTEMPT TO MAKE BULLDOG'S OATMEAL-CARROT COOKIES WITHOUT ADULT SUPERVISION.

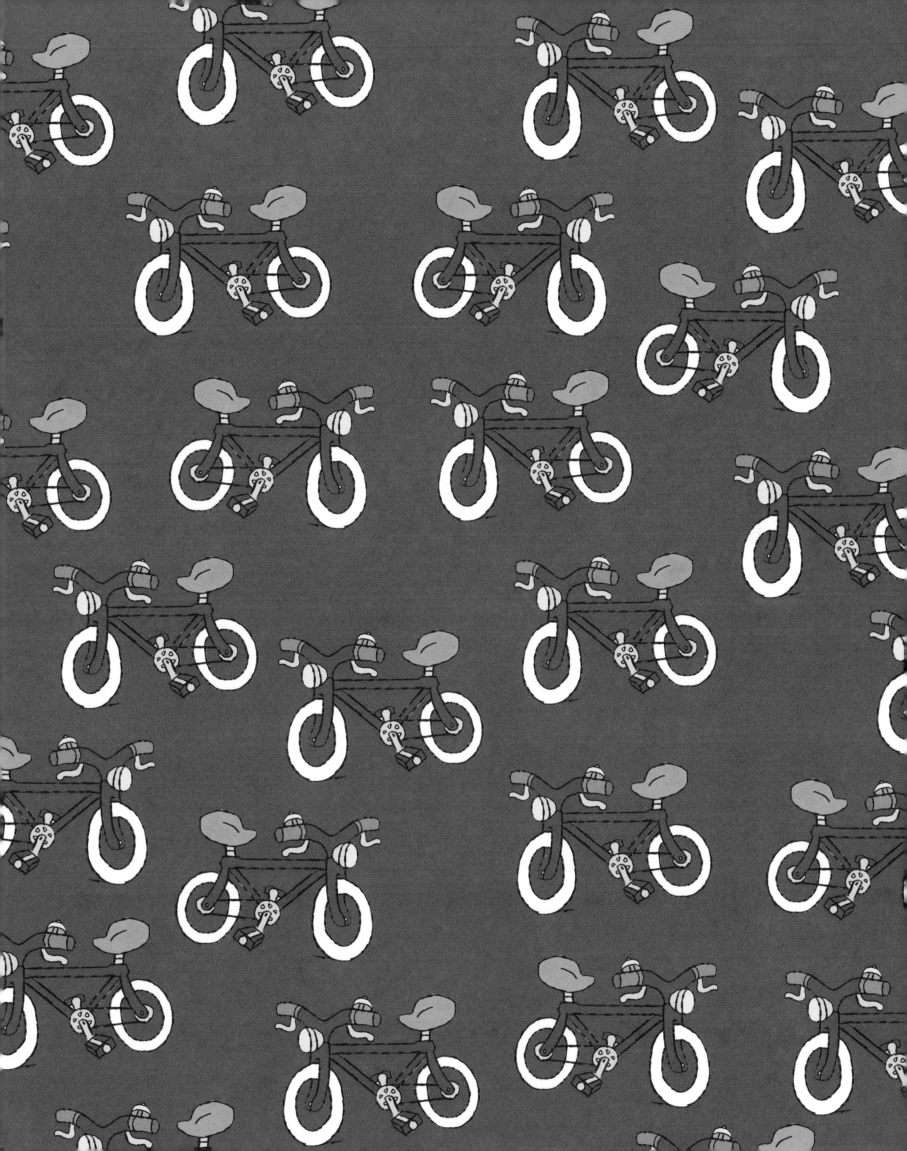

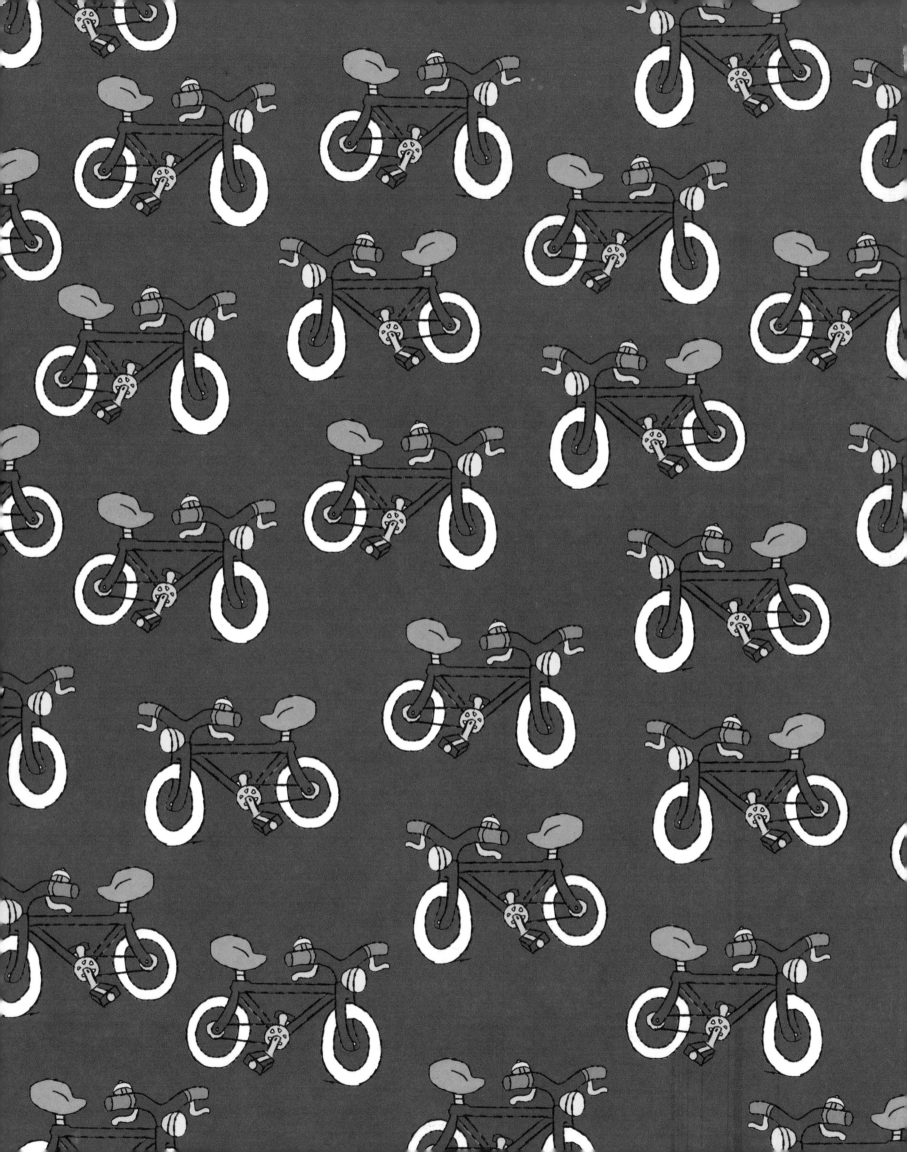